FIRST STEPS IN ORIGAMI

Origami Things with Wings

Belinda Webster

PowerKiDS press

Published in 2020 by **The Rosen Publishing Group, Inc.**
29 East 21st Street, New York, NY 10010

Cataloging-in-Publication Data

Names: Webster, Belinda.
Title: Origami things with wings / Belinda Webster.
Description: New York : PowerKids Press, 2020. | Series: First steps in origami | Includes glossary and index.
Identifiers: ISBN 9781725315006 (pbk.) | ISBN 9781725315020 (library bound) | ISBN 9781725315013 (6 pack)
Subjects: LCSH: Origami--Juvenile literature. | Paper art--Juvenile literature.
Classification: LCC TT872.5 B437 2020 | DDC 736.982--dc23

Manufactured in the United States of America

CPSIA Compliance Information: Batch CSPK20: For Further Information contact Rosen Publishing, New York, New York at 1-800-237-9932.

CONTENTS

WHAT IS ORIGAMI?

Origami is the craft of paper folding, invented in Japan hundreds of years ago. The word "origami" means "folded paper" in Japanese.

Origami paper is thin but strong, so it can be folded many times.

It is square and is usually white on one side.

You could use ordinary scrap paper instead of origami paper, but make sure it's not too thick.

BASIC FOLDS

To follow the steps in this book, there are three basic folds you need to learn.

VALLEY FOLD

To make a valley fold, fold the paper up on itself so that the crease is at the bottom, like a valley. A valley fold will be shown by a dashed line, like this.

MOUNTAIN FOLD

To make a mountain fold, fold the paper the other way, away from you. You want the crease to point up, like the peak of a mountain. We use a dotted line to show a mountain fold.

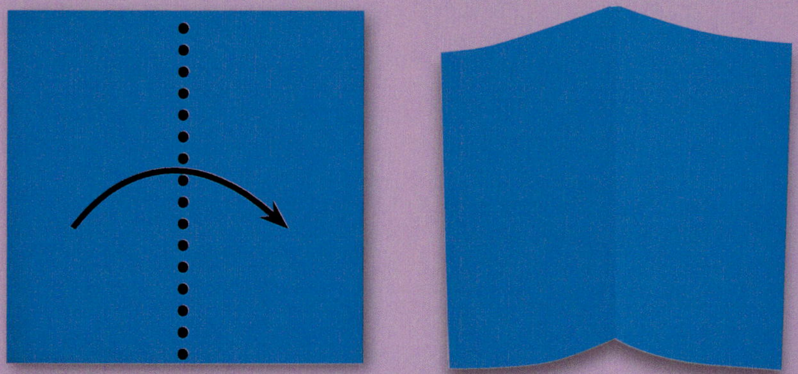

STEP FOLD

A step fold is a mountain fold and a valley fold next to each other.

1 First, make a valley fold by folding the paper up on itself so the crease is at the bottom.

2 Now unfold.

3 Next, make a mountain fold above the valley fold you have just made.

4 Push the mountain fold over the valley fold and press it flat. You now have a step fold.

KEY

- - - - - Valley fold

.... Mountain fold

Step fold

Direction to move paper

PUSH Direction to push (or pull, etc.)

SONGBIRD

This pretty songbird can be made in just a few simple steps.

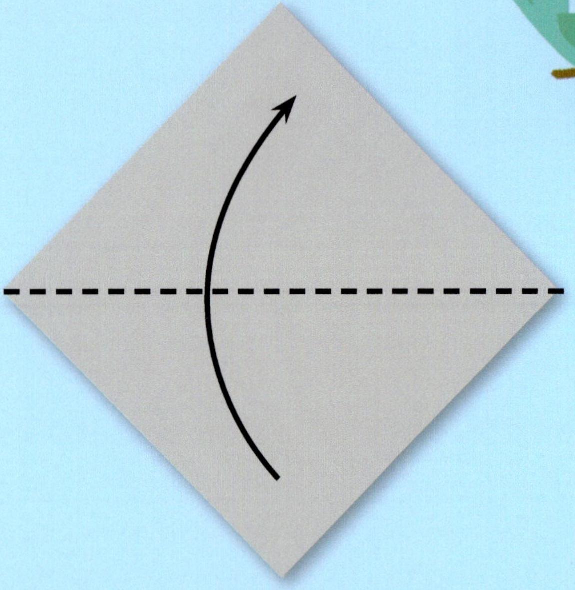

1 Start with the paper white side up, like this. Valley fold it in half, as shown. Unfold.

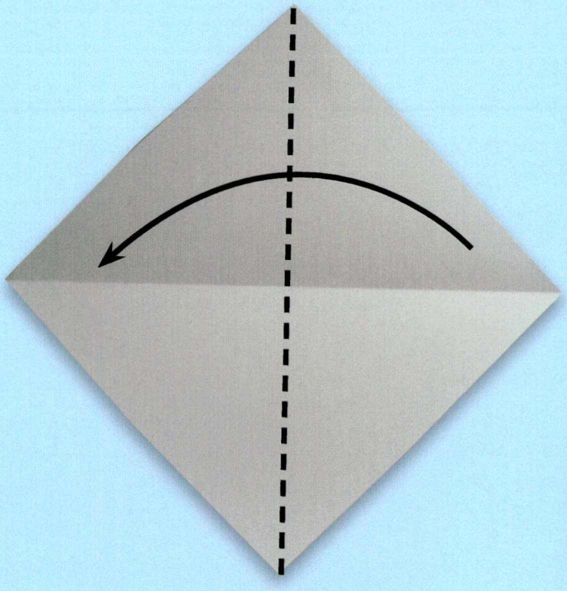

2 Valley fold it in half from right to left.

3 Valley fold the left point from left to right, as shown.

4 Valley fold the right point from right to left, as shown.

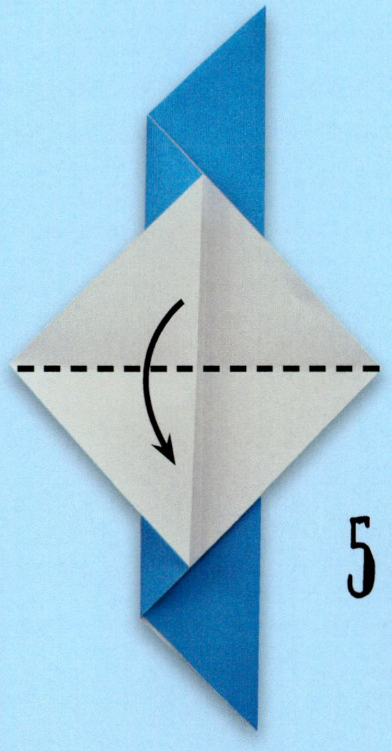

5 Open out the top flap. Valley fold the whole paper in half from top to bottom.

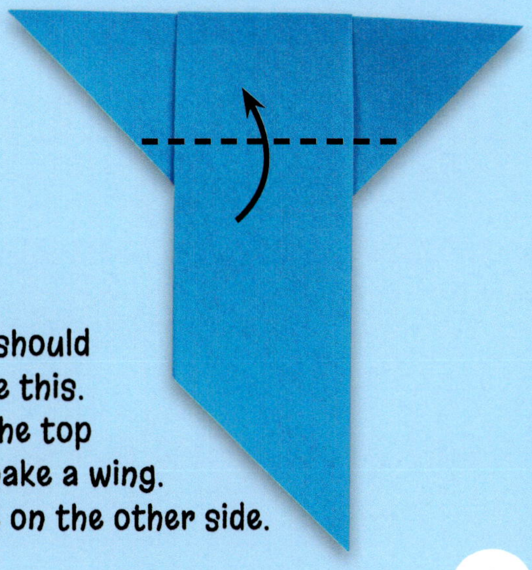

6 Your paper should now look like this. Valley fold the top flap up to make a wing. Do the same on the other side.

7 Mountain fold the left point. Unfold. Then valley fold it along the same crease. Unfold.

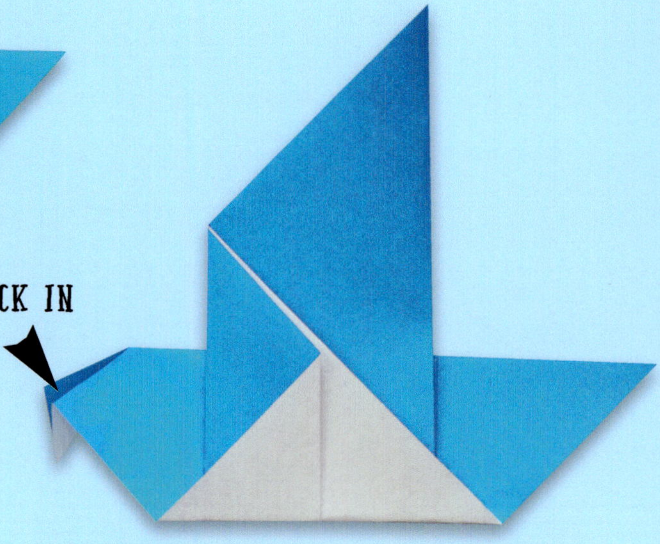

8 Tuck the left point inside the body along the crease so the tip pokes out to create the beak.

9 Gently pull out the wings. Your songbird is ready to take to the sky!

BUG

Here's how to fold a cute little bug. You could make it a spotted bug by adding dots or a striped bug by drawing lines on its back.

1 Place your paper white side up, as shown. Valley fold it in half from top to bottom.

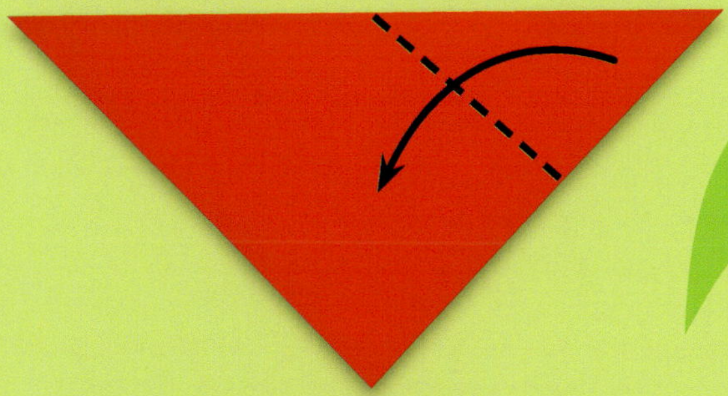

2 To create the wings, valley fold the right point so it meets the bottom point.

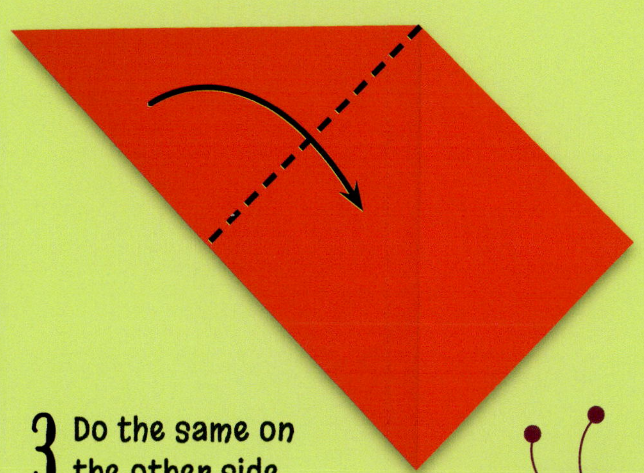

3 Do the same on the other side.

4 Your paper should now look like this. Turn it over.

5 Valley fold the top point down, as shown.

6 Valley fold the point back up.

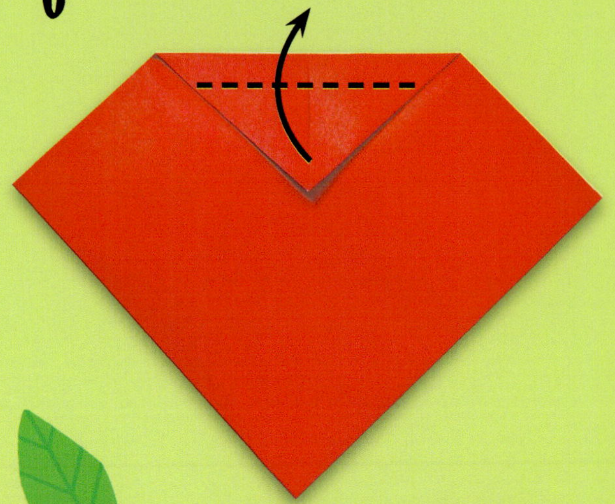

7 Valley fold the right point in, as shown.

8 Do the same on the other side.

9 Valley fold the top point down.

10 Your paper should now look like this. Turn it over.

11 Your origami bug is ready to decorate.

DRAW TWO EYES ON ITS HEAD AND A PATTERN ON ITS BACK.

BUTTERFLY

Create a beautiful origami butterfly, then make it even prettier with your pens and pencils once you've finished folding.

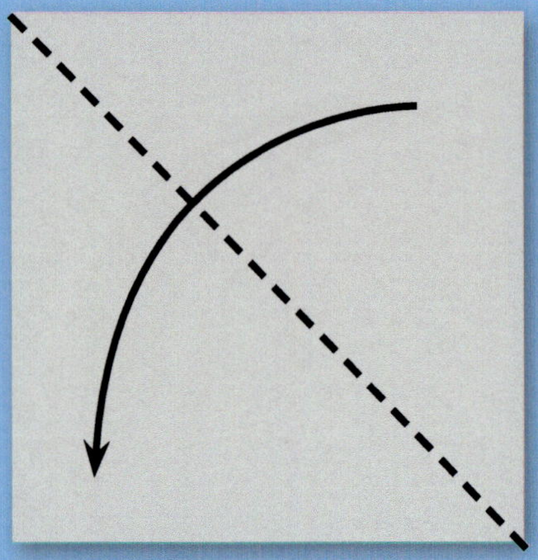

1 Start with the paper white side up, like this. Valley fold it in half diagonally, as shown. Unfold.

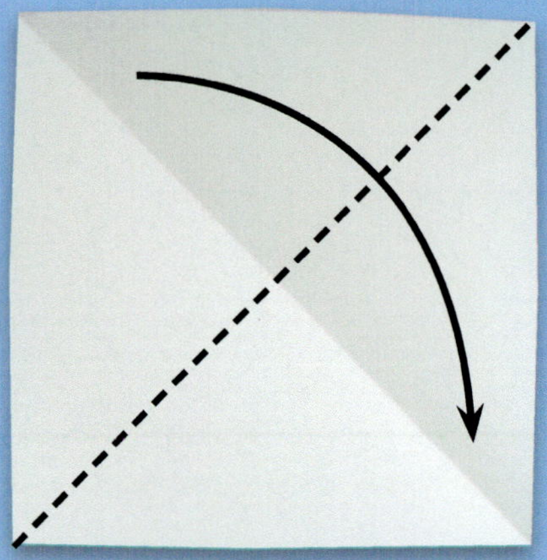

2 Valley fold the paper in half diagonally the other way. Unfold.

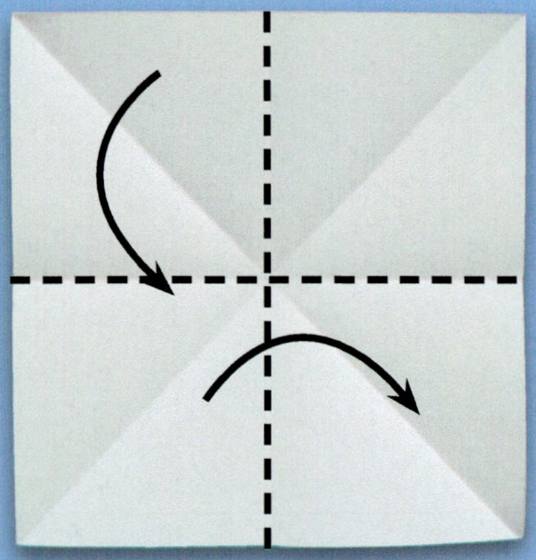

3 Valley fold the paper from top to bottom, then unfold. Valley fold it from left to right. Unfold.

4 Your paper should now look like this.

5 Valley fold the top right corner in to the middle. Valley fold the other corners in the same way.

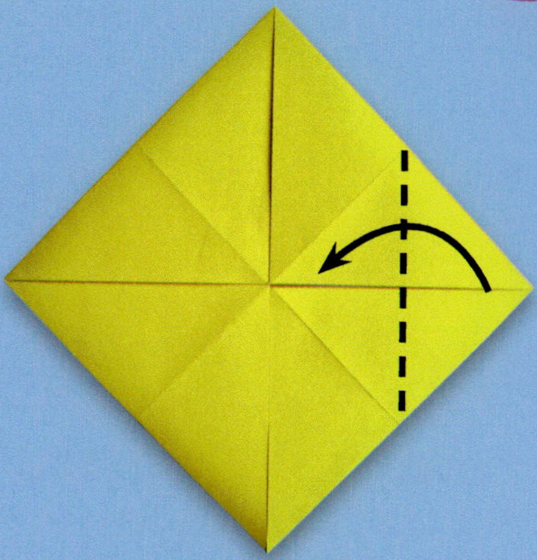

6 Valley fold the right corner in to the middle.

7 Valley fold the other corners in the same way.

8 You should now have a small square, like this.

9 Unfold your paper completely. Valley fold the right side in to the middle.

10 Valley fold the left side in to the middle.

11 Your paper should now look like this.

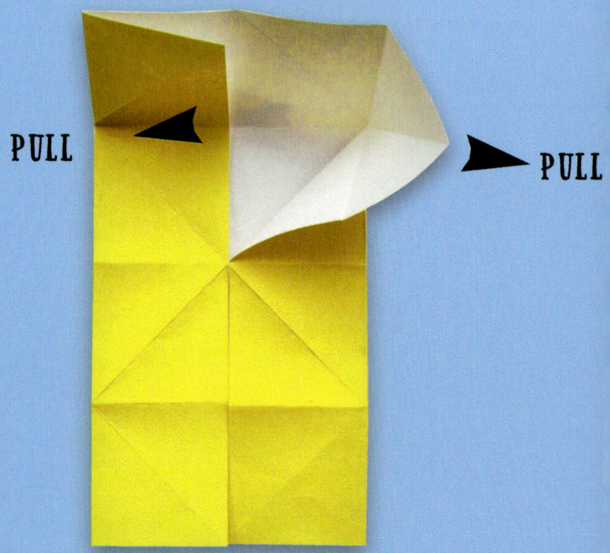

12 Gently pull the top corners open, so that the top folds down.

13 Keep pulling the corners out and bringing the top down, so that this shape appears.

14 Flatten the paper, as shown. Now rotate it, so that the top becomes the bottom.

15 Repeat steps 12 and 13 to get this shape. Mountain fold the paper in half along the middle crease.

16 Valley fold the top layer of the right point down along the diagonal crease.

17 Do the same on the other side.

18 Valley fold the top layer of the right side, as shown.

19 Do the same on the other side.

20 Valley fold the paper in half from left to right.

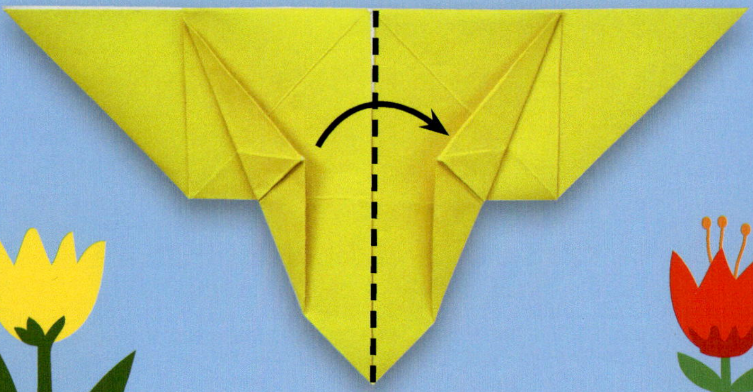

21 Mountain fold the top left corner, as shown. Unfold. Valley fold along the same crease. Unfold.

22 Bring the back layer out to the left to open out the butterfly. Pinch the folds you made in step 21 to create the butterfly's body.

GIVE YOUR BUTTERFLY SOME EYES AND PRETTY PATTERNS WITH YOUR PENS OR PENCILS.

23 Your butterfly is now finished and ready to decorate!

BUMBLEBEE

Get busy folding this friendly insect from yellow paper, then draw some black stripes with a pen.

1 Start with the paper white side up, like this. Valley fold it in half from right to left. Unfold.

2 Valley fold the paper in half from top to bottom. Unfold.

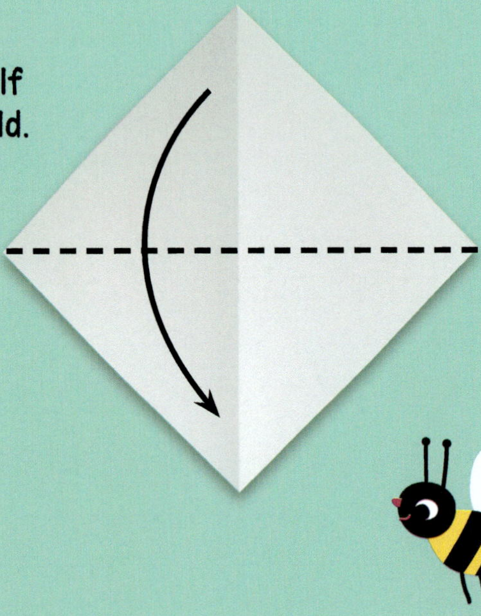

3 Valley fold the top point down, as shown, so it overlaps the central crease.

4 Mountain fold the right corner behind, as shown. The top folded edge should line up with the vertical central crease.

5 Mountain fold the left corner in the same way.

6 Valley fold the left and right corners in, as shown.

7 Your paper should look like this. Unfold the right flap.

8 Valley fold the right corner tip so the top edge meets the crease you made in step 6.

9 Your paper should now look like this. Unfold the left flap.

10 Valley fold the left corner tip so the top edge meets the crease you made in step 6.

11 Unfold the right flap and put your finger inside to open up the corner. Press it flat to make a diamond shape.

12 Now do the same on the other side.

13 Valley fold the top point down.

14 Turn over the paper. Your finished model should look like this.

NOW ADD SOME BLACK STRIPES AND A HAPPY FACE!

GLOSSARY

crease A line made by a fold.

diagonal A line in a sloping direction, from one corner to another.

mountain fold A fold where the crease points up at you, like a mountain.

songbird A kind of bird that produces musical sounds, like singing.

step fold A fold that creates a zigzag, or step, in the paper.

valley fold A fold where the crease points away from you, like a valley.

INDEX